EASY
K84me

Merry Christmas, grumpy bunny

DUERSON

DISCARD

Merry Christmas, Grumpy Bunny™

by Justine Korman  illustrated by Lucinda McQueen

Troll

For all the everyday Santas
finding ways to give their love.
—J.K.

Merry Christmas to Marissa and Benjamin.
Lots of love,
—Lucy

Text copyright © 1999 by Justine Korman.
Illustrations copyright © 1999 by Lucinda McQueen.

Published by Troll Communications L.L.C.

Grumpy Bunny is a registered trademark of Justine Korman, Lucinda McQueen,
and Troll Communications L.L.C.

Published in hardcover by BridgeWater Books.

Printed in the United States of America.
10   9   8   7   6   5   4   3

Library of Congress Cataloging-in-Publication Data

Korman, Justine.
Merry Christmas, grumpy bunny / by Justine Korman; illustrated by Lucinda McQueen.
p.   cm.
Summary: Hopper, a grumpy bunny, reluctantly agrees to play Santa
Claus at the mall and finds the job tiring but rewarding.
ISBN 0-8167-6580-4 (pbk.)
ISBN 0-8167-6270-8 (lib. bdg.)
[1. Christmas Fiction. 2. Santa Claus Fiction. 3. Rabbits Fiction.]
I. McQueen, Lucinda, ill.
II. Title.
PZ7.K83692 Md 1999

Christmas was coming! Everyone at Easter Bunny Elementary
School was full of good cheer—except Hopper. The grumpy
bunny couldn't have felt grumpier.

Hopper was tired of shopping. His feet hurt. And after buying presents for everyone else, he couldn't afford the foot massager he wanted for himself.

"No one ever gets me what I really want," Hopper grumbled. "It's always just boring sweaters and itchy socks."

And if anybunny else asked him where his holiday spirit was, Hopper was going to scream!

Suddenly, Lilac burst into the room. The pretty music teacher was excited.

"Guess who's going to be Mrs. Claus at the Bunnyburg Mall?" she said. "Me! And they still need someone to be Santa. But if they don't find somebunny soon, the mall manager will call off the performance."

Hopper could tell where this was going. And he didn't like it. "You want *me* to be Santa Claus for a bunch of whining bunnies in a crowded mall?" he asked.

Lilac smiled. And Hopper's heart melted as his sore feet throbbed. He could never say no to Lilac.

"We rehearse at eight A.M. and open at nine on Christmas Eve.
I'll take you to the manager's office. He has your Santa suit there.
Thank you so much, Hopper," Lilac said sweetly.

On Christmas Eve, the grumpy bunny wriggled into the itchy Santa costume. Lilac made a lovely Mrs. Claus. Together, they followed the busy mall manager as he quickly told them what to do.

"Basically, you sit the bunnies on your lap, one at a time, listen to what they want for Christmas, say 'ho-ho-ho,' and send them on their way," the manager said. "Any questions?"
Hopper shook his head.

They had a few minutes left before the mall opened.
Lilac used the time to recall what Santa had meant to
her when she was young.

"All year I tried so hard to be good. I did my homework and chores, and practiced the piano. It often seemed as if no one noticed—except Santa."

"Every Christmas season I waited and hoped. On that magic day,
Santa would always bring something wonderful," Lilac marveled.
"I loved to picture him in his bright red suit, so merry and kind."

Suddenly, Hopper felt proud of his itchy costume.
He was determined to be the best Santa he could be!

The doors opened, and the first arrivals came rushing up
to Hopper.

The little bunnies squealed with delight at the sight of him.
Hopper ho-ho-ho'd. This wasn't so bad. In fact, it was fun!

The grumpy bunny wasn't grumpy anymore. He had the Christmas spirit! He felt full of love and joy!

But as the hours went by, Hopper's lap got tired. His head began to ache. He found out that being Santa isn't all cookies and milk.

One bunny tugged at Hopper's beard and cried, "You're not the real Santa Claus!"

Some of the little bunnies were scared! They screamed in Hopper's ears.

Other bunnies couldn't decide
what to ask for. Hopper tried
to be patient.

"Your *ho-ho-ho* is lame!" said one visitor. Another complained, "Last year's Santa was better." Hopper sighed.

Some bunnies were rowdy, like the young twins who wanted a trampoline.

Other bunnies were downright naughty. When Hopper tried
to stop an argument, he accidentally got punched in the nose!
"Ow-ow-ow!" Santa Hopper wailed.
"That's 'ho-ho-ho,'" the manager corrected.

Through it all, Hopper tried to stay true to Lilac's image of Santa. He made sure his *ho-ho-ho*'s were merry. And he had a kind word for everybunny, even the one who sneezed on his beard.

Finally, the long day was over. Hopper dragged himself home
on his weary feet. As he neared his cozy little house, he realized
he was still wearing the Santa suit.

"Oh, bah humbug!" he griped. "I'll have to take it back to the
mall the day after Christmas."

Just then, Hopper noticed a brightly wrapped package on his doorstep. What could it be?

He read the gift tag: TO SANTA FROM SANTA. Hopper looked up. For just a moment, he thought he saw a sleigh in the sky! But when he rubbed his tired eyes, the vision was gone.

Hopper shook his head. *Maybe the package is from Lilac,* he thought.

Hopper hurried into the house and tore open the box. Inside, he found . . . a foot massager! How wonderful! For once, the grumpy bunny had received exactly what he wanted.

But it wasn't really the foot machine that made Hopper so happy. It was the feeling that Lilac had described. Someone had noticed how hard he was trying and had made a special effort to bring him the perfect reward.

Hopper put his tired feet inside the massager and sighed happily. Now he was looking forward to Christmas. He couldn't wait to give gifts to all the bunnies he loved. Just the thought of it made his belly shake with a genuine *ho-ho-ho!*

You don't need a beard or eight tiny reindeer
to spread lots of joy and Christmas cheer:
Just find the love that's deep inside,
and you'll give someone a sweet surprise!